How To Heal With Fairy Rainbow

Author Nerissa Marie

Illustrations by Snezana Grncaroska

Graphic Designs by Marccos Star

This book is dedicated to love consciousness bliss, Satcitānanda - The ever present source consciousness, the space behind the mind within the heart from where all arises. Namaste.

Title Imprints Childrens Books Kids Books and Books for Kids is an imprint of The Quantum Centre, Australia
Published by Happiness Bliss Press an imprint of The Quantum Centre, Australia

ISBN: 978-1-925647-52-5

Most Happiness Bliss Press books are available at special quantity discounts for bulk purchase for sales promotions, premiums, fund-raising, and educational needs. For details contact books@happinessbliss.com

National Library of Australia Cataloguing-in-Publication entry
Creator: Marie, Nerissa, author.
Title: How To Heal Your Chakras With Fairy Rainbow (Children's book about a Fairy, Chakra Healing and Meditation, Picture Books, Kindergarten Books, Toddler Books, Kids Book, 3-8, Kids Story, Books for Kids) Nerissa Marie (author) ; Snezana Grncaroska (illustrator) ; Marccos Star (graphic design).
ISBN: 9781925647525 (paperback)
Target Audience: For primary school age.
Subjects: Self-esteem in children--Juvenile fiction.
Self-confidence in children--Juvenile fiction.
Happiness--Juvenile fiction.
Self-actualization (Psychology) in children--Juvenile fiction.
Other Creators/Contributors: Snezana Grncaroska, illustrator.

FIRST EDITION

rologue

Each child is unique, it's important that we nurture our little ones so they may express themselves with love, light and joy. Positive thinking and affirmations helps create a space where it's safe to feel and let go. They are a wonderful way to connect to the light of our being.

When a child discovers inner peace, they become angels of love guiding those who surround them. A beautiful smile, from an innocent heart, lights up the lives of all who share in their magic. Radiating inner peace, children become strong and vibrant sharing their joy, creative natures and peaceful spirit with the world.

This story is created with the intention that your child may look within to find happiness and discover the confidence and courage to shine bright!

Whenever Fairy Rain felt sad, or embarrassed a large grey cloud would appear, hovering above her head. The more upset she became, a storm would form in the cloud and soon she'd be sopping wet!

The only real friends she had were the flowers in the meadows. Everywhere Fairy Rain went sadness was likely to follow.

One day she was sitting atop a little flower crying, when a beautiful voice said, "Hello Fairy Rain."

Standing before her stood a mysterious woman, made from nature. Flowers grew in her hair along with birds, bees, stars and trees.

"Who are you?"

"My name is Mother Earth. Why are you crying Fairy Rain?"

"I'm afraid the rain upon my head will never end. It's driving me round the bend! Maybe it's my destiny to always be wet and unhappy."

"Ah," replied Mother Earth. "I see."

W hat do you see?" asked Fairy Rain.

"Your chakras are blocked."

"What's a chakra?"

"Whirlpools of magical life-force energy. Rainbows of colour displaying your feelings and emotions. You have seven main chakras. When they are balanced you feel happy, healthy and brave. If blocked you may feel sad, scared, alone and full of guilt, blame and shame."

"Can you heal my chakras?"

"I can share with you the essence of Earth energy, to open your base chakra. Think of your fear that the rain will never cease above your head."

Focusing on her fear, Fairy Rain breathed out.

"Good, now let go." Mother Earth smiled. "You are safe, grounded and supported my child."

With a whoosh the cloud above her head blew away and at the base of her spine a beautiful red light swirled bright.

"How can I open my other chakras?"

"Follow your intuition. The universe supports your quest. A clue, to open the second chakra, visit the ones who live under the sea and sing in voices of pure harmony!"

"The mermaids!" Fairy Rain flew to the ocean shore. She sang a pretty little ditty and one soon appeared on a nearby rock.

"Hello, my name is Fairy Rain. Can you please help me open my second chakra?"

"Ah, the sacral chakra. Do you have any guilt, perhaps?" asked the mermaid in a soft voice.

"I feel guilty I spent so much time worrying about the rain cloud above my head. When I could've been helping Mother Earth instead."

"Can you forgive yourself?"

"I am open and willing to forgive myself."

The mermaid placed her hand upon Fairy Rain's tummy under her belly button. A beautiful orange light flooded through her body as Fairy Rain's second chakra opened.

With a swish and splash the mermaid dove back into the ocean.

Fairy Rain felt amazing! Wanting to open her third chakra just below her ribs she said, "Open". She felt nothing but squeezing pain. When she opened her eyes, a small red dragon floated in the air before her.

"I see you're trying to open the solar plexus chakra," the dragon spoke through puffs of smoke. "Tell me do you feel self-confident? Are you carrying any shame, perhaps?"

"I do sometimes feel ashamed of myself. I feel I am not good enough. Like I don't belong and I'm not strong."

"Are you willing to surrender the burden of your shame?" asked the dragon.

"Yes! I've always done the best I could with the knowledge I have."

The dragon roared beautiful golden fire into Fairy Rain's solar plexus chakra. The warmth of the flames filled her body, and she felt a surge of inner confidence and personal power.

The dragon disappeared with a burst of flames and in his place floated a beautiful cherub.

"I've been sent by the angels above as I love to talk about unconditional love. Have you ever felt grief?"

"My heart broke when I lost my father in a giant storm." As she remembered, sadness swept through her body. The rain cloud appeared once more above Fairy Rain's head.

"We all say goodbye to those we love at some point, but it's not really goodbye. For their love remains in our hearts until we meet again." With a flick of his arrow the cherub swished the rain cloud away. "We are made of love. It doesn't come from up above. Love is never far. Love is what you are."

Fairy Rain felt her heart glow. A green orb floated before her and love filled her heart chakra. Fairy Rain wanted to tell the world how wonderful it felt to feel love! But when she went to speak all that could be heard was a tiny squeak.

Open the fifth chakra and you'll gain the confidence to speak your truth," advised the cherub. "Visit the great reindeer in the woods. He can help." The cherub opened his wings and fluttered back to the heavens.

Fairy Rain took flight to the forests of the north. A great reindeer waited for her on the edge of the forest.

"I heard the whispers of your friend the cherub floating through the wind. Are you willing to speak what you feel to be true, kind and necessary? This will open your throat chakra."

"I like being kind. But sometimes I feel if I speak my truth, others may laugh at me or reject me."

"Your words must be chosen wisely. The throat chakra is blocked by the lies we tell ourselves. You are worthy and divine! You are more than enough. You were placed in this Earth space by sacred grace. Listen to your heart and speak from here, remember love is always near."

A bloom of blue air swirled from the reindeer's lips illuminating Fairy Rains throat chakra. "You are strong and bold may the truth of your bravery now be told!"

Fairy Rain's mind whirled. She sat on a nearby rock and closed her eyes watching her thoughts twist and twirl. A unicorn floated towards her. She opened her eyes, and the unicorn manifested.

"I'm a creature that lives upon the astral planes. I felt your presence as you became mindful of your thoughts. The universe sent me to help open your sixth chakra, the third eye. Tell me, where do you begin?"

"I begin at my nose, my toes, my... actually I'm not sure where I begin or where I end."

"You begin at the start and start at the end of time and space. There is no place where you end and I begin." The unicorn touched his forehead to Fairy Rain's and her world filled with indigo sparkling stars as her third eye awakened.

The unicorn smiled. "You've one chakra left to open, the crown chakra. Find the wise old Bodhi tree. He has let go of all attachment."

"Thank you," Fairy Rain replied.

She flew deep into forest where she found the Bodhi tree. The beautiful tree seemed to welcome her though he said not a word.

In the presence of the Bodhi tree she discovered a stillness so pure it rippled with bliss and divine consciousness. She sat at the Bodhi trees base and felt his grace. A violet light shone bright on her crown. She felt herself melt and dissolve into peace, the purity of all that exists.

"Welcome my daughter," said the Bodhi tree. "You have now set yourself free. Your crown chakra is open through unspoken awareness and bliss. You've become a rainbow of light. Your new name is Fairy Rainbow."

Then something very magical happened. All of Fairy Rainbow's chakras whirled and twirled. Fairy Rainbow felt consciousness and love fill her entire body. She felt free and joyfully happy. Her body shimmered into a beautiful, sparkling, magical rainbow.

Whenever you see a rainbow in the sky, know Fairy Rainbow is showing up to say hi, as she watches your life go by. She loves every part of you. Always remember, you have all the colours of the rainbow living inside you too.

Chakras

7th Chakra, Crown. Sanskrit Name: Sahasrara. Located just above the top of the head. Colour: Violet. Element: Nothingness, beyond. Crystal: Amethyst. Virtues: Cosmic perception, intuition and inspiration.

6th Chakra, The Third Eye. Sanskrit Name: Ajna. Located between the eyebrows, on the forehead. Colour: Indigo. Crystal: Lapis Lazuli. Element: Light. Virtue: Perception, vision, intuition, insight, inspiration and imagination.

5th Chakra, Throat. Sanskrit name: Vishuddha. Located at the throat. Colour: Blue. Element: Space/Ether. Crystals: Aquamarine & Blue Lace Agate. Virtues: Communication, sound, truth, connection and expression.

4th Chakra, Heart. Sanskrit name: Anahata. Located at the centre of the chest. Colour: Green. Element: Air. Crystals: Rose Quartz & Green Calcite. Virtues: Unconditional Love, self-love, compassion, forgiveness, relationships and sharing.

3rd Chakra, Solar Plexus. Sanskrit name: Manipura. Located just below the ribcage. Colour: Yellow. Element: Fire. Crystal: Citrine. Virtues: Transformation, will power, purpose, self-confidence and personal power.

2nd Chakra, Sacral. Sanskrit name: Svadhisthana. Located just below your belly button. Colour: Orange. Element: Water. Crystal: Carnelian. Virtues: Passion, creativity, desire, feelings.

1st Chakra, Root Chakra. Sanskrit name: Muladhara. Located at the base of the spine. Colour: Red. Element: Earth. Crystal: Red Garnet. Virtues: Trust, prosperity, physical health, stability and sense of ease in the world.

Chakra Balancing

1st Chakra, Root Chakra: Standing tall imagine yourself as a beautiful mountain. Strong, grounded and tall, reaching deep into the Earth.

2nd Chakra, Sacral: Place your hands onto your lower tummy. Feel the air swishing all around the mountain, become the air.

3rd Chakra, Solar Plexus: Resting your hands just above your belly button, see the light of the sun shining onto the mountain. Feel it's warmth filtering through the mountain and into your body.

4th Chakra, Heart: With your hands upon your chest become a beautiful flower growing atop the mountain. Become the flower warmed by the sun. Feel love fill your heart. Smile little flower and embrace fresh new growth.

5th Chakra, Throat: Bring your hands to rest lightly on your throat. Sing! "I am lovable! I love and approve of myself! It is safe to speak my truth. I am courageous."

6th Chakra, The Third Eye: Become an eagle soaring across the sky. Watching the mountain, with clear insight you can see tiny mice darting into the grass as you sweep across a sunny sky. Bring your arms, like graceful wings into prayer above your head.

7th Chakra, Crown: Become the watcher. You are the birds, the mouse, the flowers, the air, the mountain. You watch as the dream of life plays out before you, knowing you are one with all. Light fills your palms, still held high above your head and you bring this light down into your heart as you bring your hands to prayer at the centre of your chest. Love fills your entire body. You are this bliss, this grace, this divine love.

Positive Affirmations

Repeat each affirmation aloud before going to sleep for 30 days.

I am Loved

I am Safe

I am Beautiful

I am Smart

I make Friends Easily

School is Fun and Easy

I am Listened Too

I am Brave

I am a Good

I Love Myself

I am Healthy

I am Kind

I am Thankful

Mindfulness Meditation
For Inner Peace

1. Find a quiet place where you feel calm.

2. Sit with your legs crossed or find a comfy place to lay down. Gently close your eyes.

3. Squeeze your whole body, fingers, toes, knees and nose. Squish, squish, squish! Let go!

4. Take three breathes deep into your belly.

5. Feel your heart. Imagine a beautiful love heart shining in the centre of your chest. It can be any colour you like. Watch it grow and the colour of the love heart fill your body.

6. If anything or anyone has upset you, say aloud or in your mind, 'I am safe and loved.'

7. If your mind is thinking about things let it be. Just watch your thoughts.

8. Relax and feel peace. Smile!

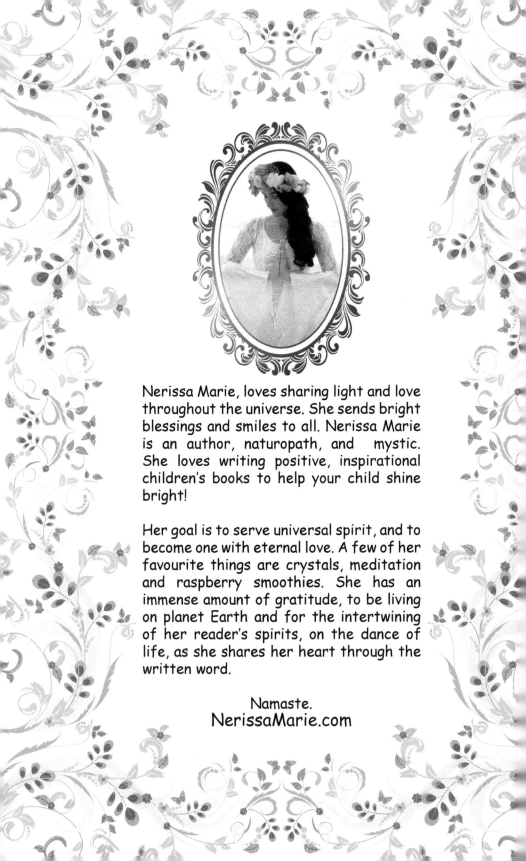

Nerissa Marie, loves sharing light and love throughout the universe. She sends bright blessings and smiles to all. Nerissa Marie is an author, naturopath, and mystic. She loves writing positive, inspirational children's books to help your child shine bright!

Her goal is to serve universal spirit, and to become one with eternal love. A few of her favourite things are crystals, meditation and raspberry smoothies. She has an immense amount of gratitude, to be living on planet Earth and for the intertwining of her reader's spirits, on the dance of life, as she shares her heart through the written word.

Namaste.
NerissaMarie.com

Positive Inspirational Children's Books

Available on Amazon and most other retailers in Hardcover, Paperback, Kindle and Epub format.

Princess Kate, loves to meditate. One day deep in bliss, she levitates high into the sky, leaving behind her friends and family. Prince Ravi Yogi arrives at the kingdom, offering to help bring Princess Kate back down to Earth. Will they listen to his advice? Or will Princess Kate, forever float above the palace, just out of reach?

This books intention is to build your child's self-esteem through a story of mindfulness meditation.

Thomas Discovers The Purpose Of Life, is an inspirational moral story encouraging your child to live a confident, happy and positive life. Thomas is a remarkable boy who questions the meaning of life. This leads him on a journey of self-discovery, where he makes new friends and discovers his life purpose. As his heart opens he connects to his inner light and becomes a sparkling beacon of joy.

This books intention is to build your child's self-esteem and self-confidence, in a happy and fun way.

FREE GIFTS! Future releases, free book promotions, and more!

Available at NerissaMarie.com

CPSIA information can be obtained
at www.ICGtesting.com
Printed in the USA
LVHW011048090221
678790LV00012B/380

9 781925 647525